Baba's Babushka

A Magical Ukrainian Easter

written by
Marion Mutala

illustrated by
Wendy Siemens

To my three children:
Symret, my spring pysanka; Natasha, my winter kolach; and Jacob-Joshua, my summer sonechko.

To my baba, Tessie Woznakowski, born in 1890 in the village or region of Zupkova in the Ukrainian province of Sokal.
And to my dido, Stefan Dubyk, who was born in 1888 in the village of Perespa, Sokal
and emigrated from Ukraine to Canada in 1912. They were married in Saskatoon, Saskatchewan in 1913.

And to the descendants of the Dubyk and Mutala families—especially my dear late sister, Evelyn Dahl,
my father, August Mutala, and my mother, Sophie Mutala (neé Dubyk), for being the special baba in my story.

Baba's Babushka: A Magical Ukrainian Easter
Text © Marion Mutala, 2012
Illustrations © Wendy Siemens, 2012

Manufactured by Friesens Corporation in Altona, MB, Canada
August 2012; November 2013
Job #90104

Library and Archives Canada Cataloguing in Publication
Mutala, Marion, 1957-
    Baba's babushka : a magical Ukrainian Easter / written by Marion Mutala ; illustrated by Wendy Siemens.

Includes some text in Ukrainian.
ISBN 978-1-894431-70-5

    1. Easter—Ukraine—Juvenile fiction. 2. Ukrainians—Social life and customs—Juvenile fiction.
I. Siemens, Wendy II. Title. III. Title: Magical Ukrainian Easter.

PS8626.U88B332 2012   JC813'.6   C2012-901187-8

Border design © www.istockphoto.com/Oksana Stuk
p. 22 "St. Vladimir Cathedral, Ukraine" © www.istockphoto.com/Adrian Beesly
Author and Illustrator photos © Bruce Blom
Edited by Heather Nickel and Lori Saigeon
Layout and design by Heather Nickel
Printed in Canada

With many thanks to Bruce Blom, Nadya Foty, Ed Klopoushak, Iris Kowalchuk, Yars Lozowchuk, Heather Nickel, Lori Saigeon,
Wendy Siemens, and Gerry and George Zerbecky for their assistance, and to my special sister, Angie Wollbaum, for her delicious *paska* recipe.

The Creative Industry Growth and Sustainability Program is made possible through funding provided to the
Saskatchewan Arts Board by the Government of Saskatchewan through the Ministry of Tourism, Parks, Culture and Sport.

Saskatchewan
Ministry of
Tourism, Parks,
Culture and Sport

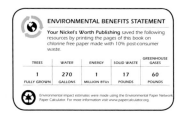

ENVIRONMENTAL BENEFITS STATEMENT
Your Nickel's Worth Publishing saved the following
resources by printing the pages of this book on
chlorine free paper made with 10% post-consumer
waste.

TREES	WATER	ENERGY	SOLID WASTE	GREENHOUSE GASES
1	270	1	17	60
FULLY GROWN	GALLONS	MILLION BTUs	POUNDS	POUNDS

Environmental impact estimates were made using the Environmental Paper Network
Paper Calculator. For more information visit www.papercalculator.org.

Your Nickel's Worth Publishing
Regina, SK.

www.yournickelsworth.com

FSC
www.fsc.org
MIX
Paper from
responsible sources
FSC® C016245

Author's Note

Ukrainian people first came to Canada during the late 1800s. *Babushka* is the Russian word for "old woman" often used to describe the headscarves worn by those early immigrants. *Fustka* [foostka] is the Ukrainian slang word for headscarf and *khustka* is the more formal spelling of the same word. When I was growing up, my family called this kind of scarf a babushka so that is the word I have used throughout.

Easter is the most important religious rite for Ukrainians, celebrating as it does the resurrection of Christ and the hope of eternal life. It is also a celebration of spring and the renewal of life.

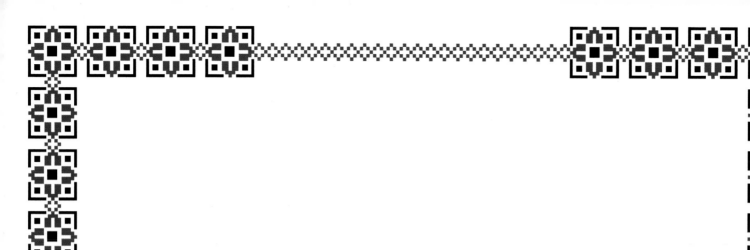

The sweet scent of blossoms near the back pond drew Natalia closer. It was an almost perfect day—the snow had melted and spring was definitely in the air. The pond behind her parents' farmhouse still had a thin crust of ice, unsafe to skate on at this time of the year, the surface slushy with water.

But as much as Natalia loved skating on the pond in winter, she especially enjoyed the spring, a time of new beginnings and many blessings, and *Velykden'*—Easter.

But Easter was much more than a celebration of spring; it was a time to remember that Jesus died on the cross and was resurrected to save people from sin. Natalia's whole family got ready for *Velykden'* or "great day." The 40-day season of Lent was a serious time of soul-cleansing and preparation. No meat was eaten on Fridays, homes were cleaned and Natalia's mother made sure that there was plenty of good food and baking ready for the Holy Day.

Natalia knelt down to get a better look at a crocus near the pond, thinking of the Easter egg she'd written on. That was her favourite part of preparing for *Velykden'*, helping her mother make *pysanky*—the special Easter eggs they wrote on with wax. Natalia liked dying the eggs different colours, yellow, orange, red and black, lightest to darkest one after the other until the final design was revealed. Her family had a collection of beautiful *pysanky*—some of them even from the old country.

As they wrote on the eggs, her mother had told her that long ago people believed that *pysanky* were magic and that the fate of the world depended upon the number of eggs decorated every Easter. According to legend, a chained-up dragon keeps track of how many eggs are made, and if one year there aren't enough, the dragon will be released and destroy everything!

Good thing Mama and I have done our part to keep the world safe for another year, Natalia thought now, giggling to herself. They'd made twenty *pysanky* already.

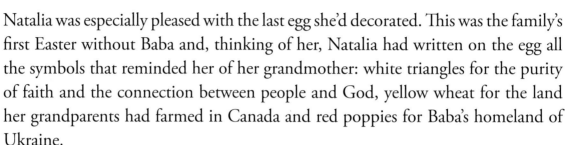

Natalia was especially pleased with the last egg she'd decorated. This was the family's first Easter without Baba and, thinking of her, Natalia had written on the egg all the symbols that reminded her of her grandmother: white triangles for the purity of faith and the connection between people and God, yellow wheat for the land her grandparents had farmed in Canada and red poppies for Baba's homeland of Ukraine.

She had added a cross to represent the resurrection and made it blue to match the sky—somehow Natalia always remembered Baba best when she looked at the wide prairie sky. Finally, she'd dipped the egg in black, giving it a solid background. Mama had told her the black meant eternity.

The egg had turned out so well, Natalia kept it in her pocket so she could look at it whenever she wanted.

Now, looking for more spring crocuses in the early morning light, she walked around to the other side of the pond. She could feel the small thud of the *pysanka* against her leg as she walked.

The willow trees were studded with soft, silky pussy willows, another sure sign of spring. Natalia chuckled a bit, thinking of last week's church service.

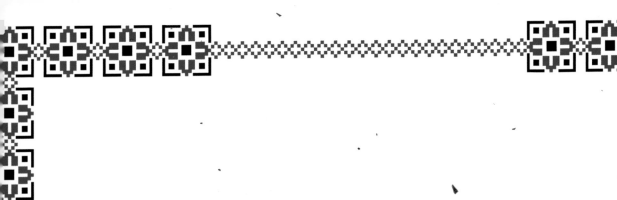

It had been Palm Sunday, *Verbna Nedilya*. Instead of palm branches, though, branches of the pussy willow tree called *loza* were blessed in church and handed out to the congregation at the end of the service.

People used the branches to tap each other gently, remembering Christ's suffering and wishing one another good health and happiness by reciting a poem that meant "the willow is hitting, I'm not hitting; one week from today, it will be Easter."

Natalia had particularly enjoyed tapping her brother Mykolai on the behind—payback for all the times he'd teased her!

Today Mama was making *pasky*, Easter bread, and Natalia could hardly wait to taste it—it was so good, the bread light and sweet. Mama decorated the top of her *paska* loaves with bits of dough shaped into crosses, suns, flowers, leaves and pine cones, representing new life and the rebirth of spring.

Every homemaker wanted her *pasky* to be the best and the most ornate, and some even believed that how this special bread turned out was a sign of the way the rest of the year would unfold. A high, beautifully golden loaf of *paska* meant a year of blessings.

While mixing the bread, Mama often prayed that her family would be happy and healthy and that the *pasky* would help nourish them for another year. Mama was known for her *pasky*; she was one of the best bakers in the town of Hafford, Saskatchewan.

Many asked Mama's advice about the art of bread-making, especially about Easter bread. No one was allowed to make loud noises while the *paska* was baking for fear it would collapse in the oven. That was why Mama had sent Natalia outside to play, promising she could help next year.

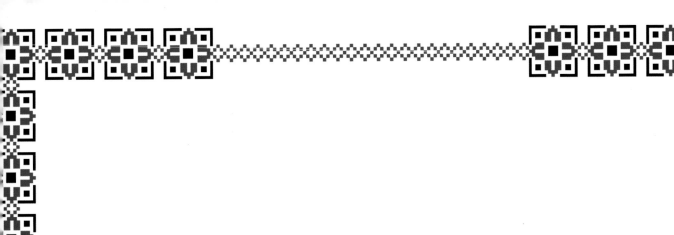

And so Natalia thought it best to stay as far away from the kitchen as possible—it was safer to be outdoors. She was on her way to collect the daily eggs from the chickens but she'd been distracted by the inviting pond to sit, watch the birds and enjoy the sunshine.

The breeze blew cool wisps of air over her and Natalia felt the first few drops of spring rain. *Duzhe dobre*, she thought, *Tato will be happy that the fields will be watered.*

Her father had just planted the wheat fields of their farm, hoping the spring rains would come soon enough to help the seeds sprout.

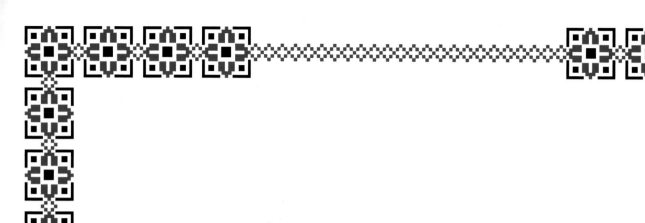

Natalia looked up into the clouds, remembering how her baba had loved this time of year. Oh, how she missed her grandmother!

She touched the egg in her pocket, thinking of all the things that had made Baba so special: the warmth of her hugs, the lip-smacking taste of her *pyrohy*, the laughing twinkle in her eyes.

The sprinkle of rain became a shower around her, but Natalia was surprised to discover that she wasn't getting wet. Instead of fat raindrops, Natalia felt the petals of spring blossoms brush against her cheeks, shaping themselves into a babushka that covered her hair and warmed her ears despite the brisk breeze.

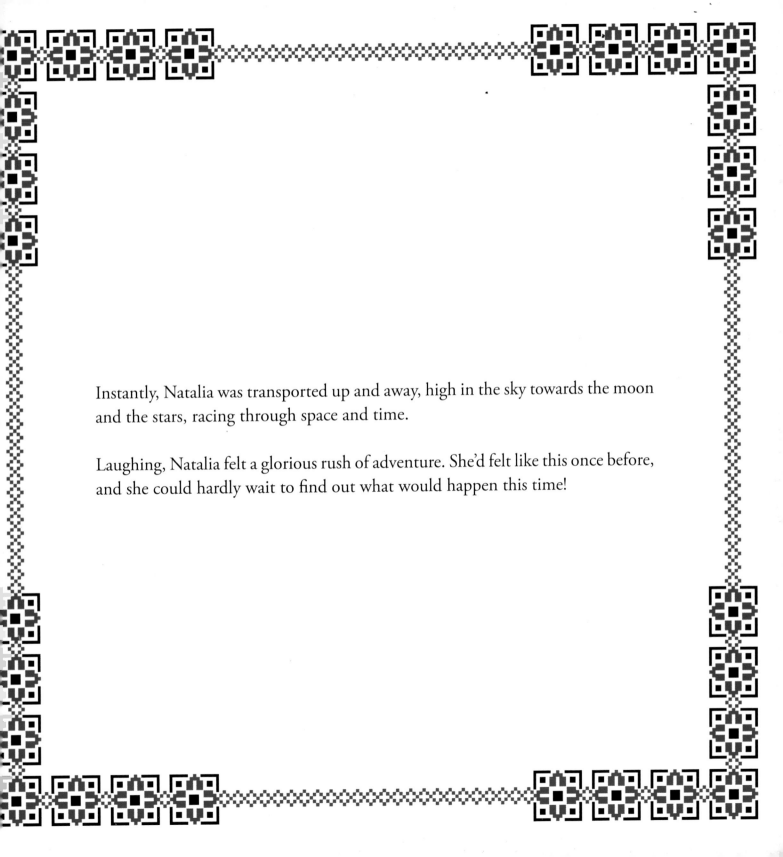

Instantly, Natalia was transported up and away, high in the sky towards the moon and the stars, racing through space and time.

Laughing, Natalia felt a glorious rush of adventure. She'd felt like this once before, and she could hardly wait to find out what would happen this time!

When the stars faded away, she found herself in a throng of people carrying candles in front of a village church, its bells ringing. Led by the priest in the darkness of early morning, she joined the procession of people singing *"Khrystos voskres!* He is risen!"

She knew they would circle the building three times to represent the Trinity. The church's closed doors were a reminder of the sealed tomb of Christ and the three days between His death and resurrection.

As she walked with the villagers, Natalia looked at the church and the village square carefully, growing more excited with each passing moment.

Could it be? Had she come back to Ukraine? Maybe she would see…

Her train of thought was interrupted when they reached the front of the church for the third time, and the priest called out, *"Khrystos voskres!"*

The people responded, *"Voistynu voskres!* He is truly risen!"

Suddenly, the church doors were flung wide to let the people in for the Resurrection Liturgy, and Natalia gaped at the blaze of candles and bright colours within. In the light of the rising sun, the transformation from dark church to colourful celebration was truly magical, and a rush of feeling filled Natalia with awe.

"Tak, voistynu voskres!" she thought to herself as she entered the church.

Once seated, Natalia glanced around, looking closely at the faces around her. She noticed all the women in church wore head coverings. Out of respect, Natalia pulled her babushka up over her own head too.

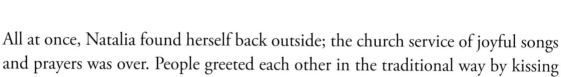

All at once, Natalia found herself back outside; the church service of joyful songs and prayers was over. People greeted each other in the traditional way by kissing each other three times—*khrystosuvannia*.

Natalia watched the commotion with delight; she was *sure* she remembered this village church from last *Sviat Vechir*. She craned her neck, hoping to see…and there she was: the girl who would someday grow up to be her baba!

Natalia edged through the throng to get closer. She was surprised to find she had to look up to see Baba's face. Baba was no longer the little girl Natalia had seen Christmas Eve; she was taller, more grown up, almost a young lady now.

Baba was lovely!

Natalia stood close to her baba's family, knowing from her last adventure that she wouldn't be detected, and waited for her favourite part of Easter Sunday morning: the blessing of the Easter baskets.

Each family had brought to church a basket containing a *paska* wrapped in an embroidered cloth, along with a few other foods like cheese, ham or *kovbasa* (sausage), horseradish, salt, *krashanky* (coloured eggs) and, of course, the beautiful *pysanky* Baba had made with her mother. In the middle of the *paska*, a candle burned brightly.

Natalia looked at the basket her baba's mother had prepared. She was glad to see it was brimming with food. The paska looked delicious and Natalia's stomach gurgled in anticipation. *Is that the same recipe my mother uses now?* she wondered, eyeing the round golden loaf with speculation as the priest blessed their basket.

It seemed there were rows and rows of baskets to be blessed by the priest. The silence was awe-inspiring. Finally, it was done and the priest shouted joyfully three more times, "*Khrystos voskres!* Christ is risen!" and everyone exclaimed loudly in reply, "*Voistynu voskres!* He has Truly Risen!"

Everyone glowed with happiness. Families laughed and hugged each other tightly. But Baba's attention wasn't on her relatives; her gaze had been caught by that of a handsome, blue-eyed young man.

Natalia watched, wide-eyed, as Baba, her sparkling eyes never leaving the boy's, slid her hand into the Easter basket and pulled out a delicate *pysanka*.

It trembled on Baba's nervous fingertips and Natalia understood that Baba had made it herself for just this moment, writing on it in wax, then dipping the fragile shell in a rainbow of colours before oh-so-carefully blowing out the egg's insides.

Baba's going to give it to that boy! Natalia realized. *She must really like him!*

But her baba must have been more nervous than even Natalia could see because the moment Baba took a step forward, the egg toppled from her hand, landing on the hard ground with an audible *cra-a-ack!*

Tears filled Baba's eyes as she looked from the ruined egg to the boy.

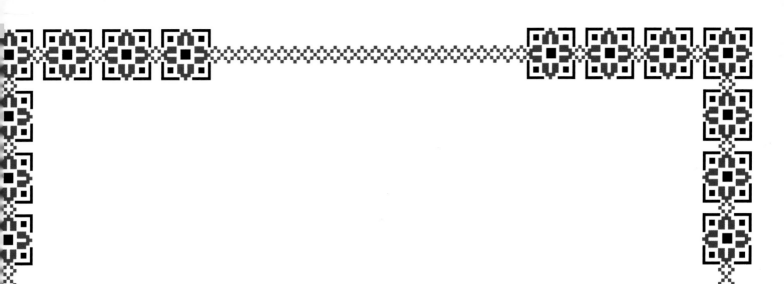

Natalia knew just what to do. She put her hand in her pocket. Taking out the precious *pysanka* she'd made, she tucked it into a tuft of grass beside the broken shell. Just as she was wondering how she'd get Baba to notice, a breeze bent the blades of grass, revealing the hidden egg.

Baba picked it up, the astonishment on her face fading as she cradled it in her hand. She glanced at the boy again. Gathering her courage, she reached for his hand and set it gently on his palm.

A grin grew wide on his face and he put the egg carefully into his family's basket as if he thought it were precious too.

Then some of the girls began to sing. Ducking her head shyly, Baba accepted the young man's hand, his sandy hair flopping down over his forehead in a way that seemed awfully familiar to Natalia.

The boy blushed as his fingers touched Baba's and Baba smiled as they joined a group of young people to dance *hahilky* in front of the church.

Natalia could feel the warmth between them and she glanced up at her great-grandparents to see what they thought of this. The twinkle in their eyes suggested that this young man was well liked by the family, and they clapped in time to the rhythm of the dance.

As he swung Baba around in the dance, it seemed to Natalia that the last chill of winter was chased away. Spring had finally arrived.

The young people sang and danced, imitating the planting and growing of crops, their actions showing their hopes for a bountiful harvest to come.

Natalia couldn't help it—the tune was so lively!—and before she knew it, she was dancing too, following Baba's steps the best she could. As she did, the babushka fell around her shoulders, unnoticed.

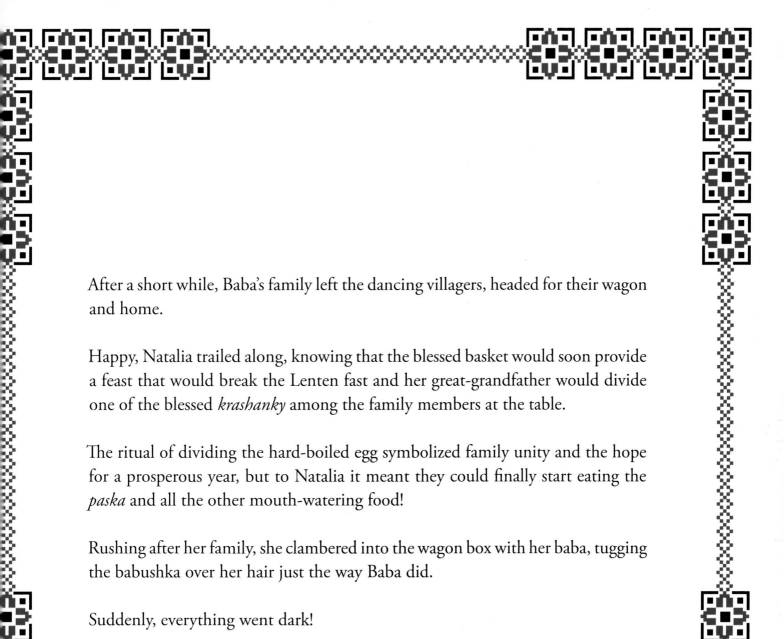

After a short while, Baba's family left the dancing villagers, headed for their wagon and home.

Happy, Natalia trailed along, knowing that the blessed basket would soon provide a feast that would break the Lenten fast and her great-grandfather would divide one of the blessed *krashanky* among the family members at the table.

The ritual of dividing the hard-boiled egg symbolized family unity and the hope for a prosperous year, but to Natalia it meant they could finally start eating the *paska* and all the other mouth-watering food!

Rushing after her family, she clambered into the wagon box with her baba, tugging the babushka over her hair just the way Baba did.

Suddenly, everything went dark!

She was awakened when someone shook her arm.

"Natalia, get up! Why are you sleeping by the pond?" her brother asked. "You've been outside all afternoon and Mama needs you to help get the Easter basket ready for tomorrow."

Natalia rubbed her eyes, looking up with astonishment at Mykolai and then down at the green babushka clutched in her hand.

"Mama let me make the *krashanky* today," he called to her as he headed back to the farmhouse, "and I know which one will beat any egg you pick!"

The thought of her brother winning their traditional egg battle was enough to make Natalia jump to her feet. She chased after him, the babushka in her hand forgotten for the moment.

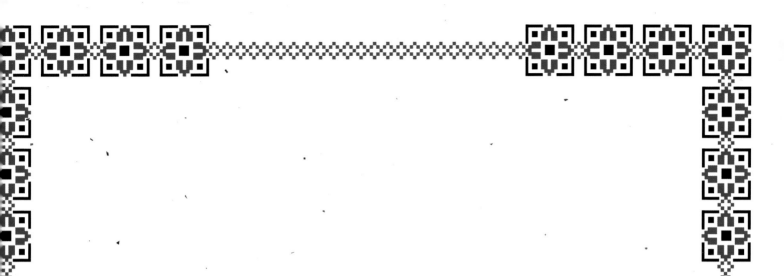

Later that night, though, as she folded the new babushka into the wooden keepsake box that had once been Baba's, Natalia thought about her grandmother and the young man she'd given the *pysanka* to.

What would have happened if I hadn't been there to help? she wondered, fingering the bright babushka before closing the lid. She knew in her heart that her grandmother had once again given her a precious gift of love and that one day they would see each other again.

She couldn't wait for the next adventure!

Ukrainian Glossary

Baba – [**bah**-bah] old woman, grandmother
Babushka – [bah-**bush**-kah] headscarf
Dido – [**dyee**-doh] grandfather
Duzhe dobre – [**doo**-zheh **doh**-breh] very good
Hahilky – [hah-**heel**'-**keh**] traditional dances, songs,
          games and dramas
Khrystosuvannia – [khreh-stohs'-oo-**vah**-nyah]
          kissing each other three times
Khrystos voskres! – [khreh-**stos**' voh-**skrass**] Christ is risen!
Khustka, Khustky – [**khoost**-kah, khoost-**keh**] scarf, scarves
Kubasa – [koo-bah-**sah**] sausages
Krashanky – [**krah**-shahn-keh] coloured eggs

Loza – [loh-**zah**]willow branches
Paska – [**pahs**-kah] Easter bread
Pyrohy – [peh-roh-**heh**] perogies
Pysanky – [**peh**-san'-keh] decorated Easter eggs
Sviat Vechir – [**svee**-at' va-**cheer**] Christmas Eve
          (literally: Holy Night)
Tak – [**tahk**] yes
Tato – [**tah**-toh] father
Voistynu voskres! – [voh-**yee**-steh-noo voh-**skrass**]
          He is truly risen!
Velykden' – [va-**lehk**-dan'] Great Day, Easter Sunday
Verbna Nedilya – [**verb**-nah ne-**deel**'-yah] Palm Sunday
          (literally, Willow Sunday)

References

"Easter—Velykden'." BRAMA - Gateway Ukraine. http://www.brama.com/art/easter.html. Accessed July 24, 2011.
Encyclopedia of Ukraine. University of Toronto Press. 1984–1993.

"Pysanka." http://en.wikipedia.org/wiki/Pysanka. Accessed August 1, 2011.

Tanya Avramenko. "Ukrainian Easter (Velykden) Traditions." *Multicultural Aged Care*. http://www.mac.org.au/docs/NLV311.pdf. Accessed July 24, 2011.

"The Joy of Resurrection in a Traditional Ukrainian Easter service—Khrystos Voskres!" http://aussiethule.blogspot.com/2006/04/joy-of-resurrection-in-traditional.html. Accessed July 24, 2011.

"Ukrainian Easter." http://web.mac.com/lubap/Ukrainian_Easter/Traditions.html. Accessed July 24, 2011.

Paska Recipe

2 packages of instant yeast (6 teaspoons)	1¼ cup sugar
4 cups scalded, then cooled milk	1½ teaspoon salt
2 cups water (optional: add 2 drops yellow food dye)	5 well beaten eggs
1½ cup oil	18 cups flour

Put white flour in a large bowl. Stir in instant yeast and mix. Put milk, water (with food colouring), oil, sugar, salt and beaten eggs in another bowl and stir. Make a well in flour and add liquid mixture. Mix and knead well. Oil the dough lightly and place in a large bowl, covering with a clean tea towel. Let rise for 1 hour in warm place. Knead down. Let rise another hour. Grease 6 pans (use 9" round cake pans or coffee tins—if using coffee tins, ball of dough should fill ½ can). Make small crosses, doves, rosettes to decorate bread on top. For 9" round cake pans, roll two or three 24" pieces of dough into ropes and braid together (double or triple braid) Place braid around inside edge of pan. Repeat with second double or triple braid and place in centre of pan. Let bread rise 1 hour and brush top of bread with beaten egg before baking. Preheat oven. Bake at 350° C for 30-40 minutes. Enjoy! Makes 6 loaves.